For my grandchildren, Oscar & Isla.
H.B.

For Amos, Elias, and Hannah, my three TechTots. Stay curious – the world is wide and full of wonder.
M.H.

First published in North America in 2019
by Boxer Books Limited.
www.boxerbooks.com

Library of Congress Cataloging-in-Publication Data available.

The illustrations were prepared digitally.
The text is set in Futura and Gliny.

ISBN: 978-1-912757-08-4
1 3 5 7 9 10 8 6 4 2
Printed in China
All of our papers are sourced from managed forests and renewable resources.

All activities featured in the TechTots series must be supervised by an adult.

WHY do things fall DOWN?

Harriet Blackford
Illustrated by Mike Henson

BOXER BOOKS

The TechTots are throwing
balls up into the air.

"I'm not very good at catching," says Oscar.

"The balls always fall back down again," says Isla.

"But what if they didn't?" asks Seb.

"What if they
kept going?"
Look
out!

"Everything falls down to the ground when you let go of it," says Oscar. "Something must pull everything down."

"Yes," says Mia. "This 'pull' is a very important thing. It's called 'gravity' and without it we wouldn't be able to walk. We'd float away!"

Wheeee!

"Let's see if we can play with gravity," says Mia. "I'll show you how to make a paper plane and we can have a race!"

1. Fold the paper in half and open it out again.

4. Repeat steps 2 and 3 on the left-hand side.

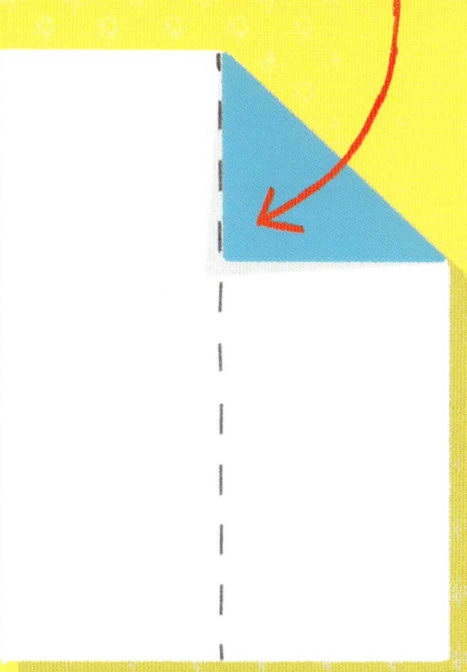

2. Fold the top-right corner to the middle.

3. Fold it over again.

5. Fold the plane in half, right to left.

6. Fold one side down to make a wing. Repeat on the other side.

Ready with your airplanes, TechTots!

Throw them hard so they beat gravity.

Wheeeeeeeeeeee

"Why did they go so far?" asks Seb.

"You pushed them," explains Mia. "Gravity pulled them down when they ran out of 'push'."

"But why don't birds fall down?" asks Oscar.

"Ahh!" says Isla. "Birds can fly because they have wings and strong muscles to keep their wings flapping."

"And what about airplanes?" asks Mia. "Their wings don't flap, do they?"

"No, they don't. They have wings to give them lift and engines to keep pushing them forward," says Seb.

"Is there anywhere you can float around without falling down?" wonders Oscar.

"Yes,
space!
You'd float there!"
shouts Seb.

"Astronauts need a rocket pack to move around."

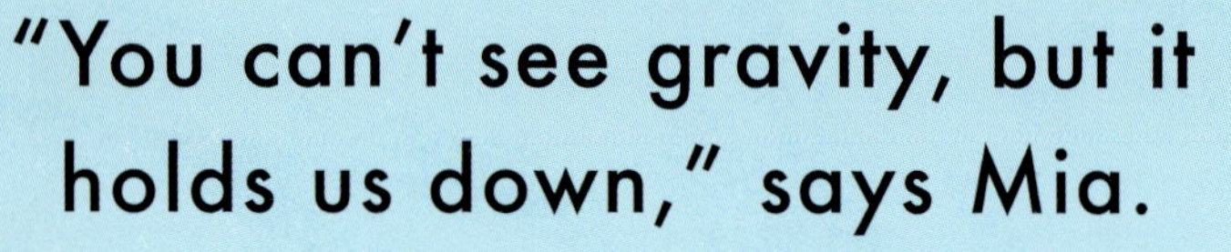

"You can't see gravity, but it holds us down," says Mia.

"It keeps our feet on the ground and everything else too."

Open

"Without gravity, everything would be floating around!" says Seb with a laugh.

Closed
Huh?
Woof!